WAY PAST JEALOUS

Hallee Adelman

illustrated by Karen Wall

Albert Whitman & Company
Chicago, Illinois

To David and all kids everywhere:
you are the Star of the Week by just being you!—HA

To all those who don't let jealousy get
in the way of friendship—KW

Library of Congress Cataloging-in-Publication data is on file with the publisher.

Text copyright © 2021 by Hallee Adelman
Illustrations copyright © 2021 by Albert Whitman & Company
Illustrations by Karen Wall
First published in the United States of America in 2021 by Albert Whitman & Company
ISBN 978-0-8075-8678-5 (hardcover)
ISBN 978-0-8075-8676-1 (ebook)

Printed in China
10 9 8 7 6 5 4 3 2 1 WKT 24 23 22 21 20

Design by Rick DeMonico

For more information about Albert Whitman & Company,
visit our website at www.albertwhitman.com.

I made my best picture ever,
but nobody noticed.
Debby drew a dog,
and everyone loved it.
I felt jealous.

So I hid my picture
and tried to draw like Debby.
"I love your bumblebees, Yaz."
I whispered, "They're not bumblebees."

Debby drew more dogs.
"What special pups!" Miss Pimmy said.
Now I was really jealous.

Miss Pimmy hung one of Debby's drawings
on the board for the Stars of the Week.
How come Miss Pimmy didn't hang
my picture this time?
Why is Debby getting all the attention?

I was way past jealous. The kind of jealous that makes you feel bad, think ugly, and act mean.

At recess, Skitter, Jin, and Nelly
huddled around Debby.
"Can you draw a dog on my hand?"
"Will you make one on my paper?"

I squinted my eyes
and stormed past them.
I felt small,
like those dogs.

I drew Debby's picture torn up on the floor.
I drew the board
for the Stars of the Week
with MY picture on it—
and everyone crowded around *me*!

"How did you do that?"
"Can you show me?
"Can you make one for me?"

When Debby saved me a seat at lunch,
I sat far away from her.
My jealousy followed me anyway.

"Look! My dog's like Debby's!" Juan said.
"Mine too," said Hooper.
I spilled my drink on purpose.
"Sorry," I said.
I wasn't sorry.

I sneaked into Miss Pimmy's room
and yanked Debby's picture down.

After lunch, Debby walked in.
"Oh! My picture is gone!"
She looked sad. Really sad.
My stomach sank.

All afternoon I looked at the board,
right where her picture used to be.
Right where I'd wanted mine to go.
Right where everyone would see it.

And I didn't feel so good.

After school I pulled Debby's picture
out of my pocket.
"Why do you have that?"
I swallowed hard and said,
"I'm sorry. I was jealous of you."

Debby's eyes got teary.
"That's mean."
She stomped away.

So I headed home, all alone.
My jealousy ruined everything.

I tried not to cry, but I couldn't help it.
"What's wrong?"
I told Dad what I did.

"Sounds like a rough day." His hug felt warm.
"What are you going to do now?" he asked.

I didn't know.

My finger traced my picture—
the friends holding hands.
It *was* my best one ever!

But I didn't want it on the board.
And I didn't want to be a Star of the Week.
I wanted Debby to be my friend again.

My stomach jittered
when I saw Debby the next morning.
I took a deep breath.
"I'm sorry I hurt your feelings."
I handed her my picture.

"Friends?" I asked.
"Friends," she said back. "I love this drawing.
And those bumblebees are so cute."

"Actually," I said, "they're supposed to be dogs."
"Bumbledogs?"
We laughed loud. It felt good.

I held out my markers.
Debby took a few.

Together we drew and drew...

And we both felt like stars.